Space Dog the Hero

by Natalie Standiford

illustrated by Kathleen Collins Howell

A STEPPING STONE BOOK™

Random House New York

For Jim-bones

www. randomhouse.com/kids

Library of Congress Cataloging-in-Publication Data
Standiford, Natalie.
Space Dog the hero / by Natalie Standiford ; illustrated by Kathleen Collins
Howell. p. cm.
"A Stepping Stone book." SUMMARY: Space Dog, who is really an alien from the
planet Queekrg, has a hard time pretending to be a watchdog when Roy's father
goes away on a business trip.
ISBN 0-679-88906-X (pbk.). — ISBN 0-679-98906-4 (lib. bdg.)
[1. Watchdogs—Fiction.   2. Dogs—Fiction.   3. Extraterrestrial beings—Fiction.]
I. Howell, Kathleen Collins, ill.   II. Title.   PZ7.S78627Sr   1999   [Fic]—dc21
97-26680

Printed in the United States of America   10 9 8 7 6 5 4 3 2 1

Contents

1
Space Dog
Sees Trouble Coming

It was early in the fall. One night before dinner, Roy Barnes sat in his room doing homework. He was having trouble concentrating. It was only the second week of school, but his teacher was already going to give a spelling test.

Roy's dog, Space Dog, was asleep nearby. He was napping on the bottom part of Roy's bunk bed.

Rrring! Suddenly the alarm clock went off. The noise of the alarm filled the room, but Space Dog didn't move.

At last Roy got up and switched off the alarm. Then he shook Space Dog.

"Hey, buddy!" said Roy. "Wake up!"

Space Dog opened his eyes. "Huh?" he said.

"Boy, are you a sound sleeper!" said Roy. "Didn't you hear the alarm?"

"No," said Space Dog. "But if it went off, that means it's dinnertime. I set the alarm so my stomach would have a little time to wake up and get really hungry."

"It's *almost* dinnertime," said Roy. He went back to his desk.

"What are you doing?" asked Space Dog.

"Trying to study," said Roy. "I have a spelling test tomorrow, and I don't know these words."

"I'll quiz you," said Space Dog. "That'll help." He took Roy's spelling book from the desk and sat on the bed. He looked at the word list and read, "Bicycle."

Roy closed his eyes. Then he said, "B-I-C-Y-C-L-E."

"Right," said Space Dog. "So what are you worried about? That's the hardest word on the list."

Most dogs don't help kids with their homework. But Space Dog wasn't really a dog. He just looked like one. He grew up on the planet Queekrg, far out in space. He was sent on a mission from Queekrg to study the planet Earth. He crash-landed in Roy's backyard, and he and Roy became fast friends. Roy was the only person who knew Space Dog's true identity.

While Roy was spelling "automobile,"

someone knocked on the door of his room. Space Dog quickly slid off the bed and sat in a doggy way on the floor.

"Come in," Roy said once Space Dog was settled.

Roy's father opened the door. "Supper's ready," he said.

"I'm coming," said Roy.

Mr. Barnes went downstairs. Roy got up from his desk.

"Save me some dessert," Space Dog said.

"Okay," said Roy, and he went downstairs to dinner.

"Don't you have something you want to tell Roy, dear?" said Mrs. Barnes. She passed the pork chops to her husband.

"Yes, I do," said Mr. Barnes. "Roy, I

have to go away on business."

"Where?" said Roy.

"To Cleveland," said Mr. Barnes. "But it's only for a few days. There's nothing to worry about."

"I'm not worried," said Roy.

"Roy, honey, you don't have to be brave with us," said Mrs. Barnes. "It's natural to be a little scared after your home has been broken into. Especially if you know your father isn't going to be around."

Then Roy knew what his parents were talking about. A few weeks before, while the Barneses were visiting Roy's granny, their house had been broken into. At least that's what Mr. and Mrs. Barnes thought had happened. The real story was that Space Dog had turned the house upside down. He had been left home alone for a few days and had made a real mess of things.

"Oh, Dad," said Roy. "I don't think there will be another burglar."

"I hope you're right, Roy," said Mr. Barnes. "But somebody else's house was broken into last week. It was in the paper."

"No kidding!" said Roy. "Were they real burglars?"

"Of course they were real," said Mr. Barnes. "That's why I'm nervous about you and your mother being alone while I'm gone. And that's why I came up with an idea."

"What kind of idea?" asked Roy.

"A very practical idea," said Mr. Barnes. "We've got a dog in the house, right?"

Suddenly Roy *was* worried. "Yes," he said slowly.

"Well," said Mr. Barnes, "why not put him to work? He can be our watchdog. He'll guard the house while you and your mother are asleep."

Roy dropped his fork. "Space Dog won't like that," he said. "I mean, he's probably not very good at watchdogging."

Mr. Barnes's face began to turn red. "Listen, Roy," he said sternly. "That animal costs me a fortune in dog food. It's time he made himself useful around here."

Roy wanted to tell his father the truth about Space Dog, but he held his tongue. Space Dog never ate a bite of the dog food that the Barneses bought. He ate people food. Roy secretly threw the dog food away.

"But Space Dog doesn't know how to be a watchdog," said Roy, still hoping to change his father's mind.

"We'll have to teach him," said Mr. Barnes. "Go to the library and see what you can find."

"I'm sure Space Dog will do fine," said Mrs. Barnes. "Protecting people comes naturally to dogs."

Roy swallowed hard. A lot of things came naturally to Space Dog, but protecting Earth people wasn't one of them.

In his room after supper, Roy broke the news to Space Dog. Space Dog did not like Mr. Barnes's idea. "I have to do *what?*" he asked, hoping he had not heard correctly.

"Guard the house at night," Roy repeated.

"This is terrible," said Space Dog. "I don't know the first thing about guarding a house. And besides, I'm as scared of burglars as your father is."

"Just give it a try," Roy pleaded. "Who knows? Maybe you'll turn out to be a lean, mean watchdog machine."

"Sure," said Space Dog. "And you're the Queen of England."

2

A Burglar's Worst Enemy

The next day was Friday. Roy went to school and passed his spelling test with flying colors. He also checked out a book from the library. It was called *How to Turn Your Dog into a Burglar's Worst Enemy.*

He walked home from school with his friend Alice. Alice lived next door. She had a poodle named Blanche. Alice loved her dog.

Roy thought Blanche was okay, but Space Dog couldn't stand the sight of her. Blanche had a crush on Space Dog.

"Guess what I have to do tomorrow," said Roy.

"What?" asked Alice.

"I have to train Space Dog," said Roy.

"He's already trained," said Alice.

"I don't mean that kind of training," said Roy. "I have to train him to be a watchdog."

"You do?" said Alice. "Why?"

"My dad is going away on a business trip," said Roy. "He's worried about burglars."

"My parents worry about burglars, too," said Alice. "But I know Blanche will protect us."

"Blanche wouldn't be a good watchdog," said Roy. "She's too friendly."

"She's friendly to *nice* people," said Alice. "But she has good instincts. She knows when someone isn't nice. I guess all dogs are like that. Isn't Space Dog?"

"Space Dog knows if people aren't nice," said Roy. "But he never growls or barks. I don't think a burglar would be afraid of him."

"There must be a little watchdog in him," said Alice. "Doesn't he ever chase squirrels or growl at other dogs?"

"Never," said Roy.

"Well," said Alice, "I hope no one ever breaks into your house."

"Me, too," said Roy.

Mr. Barnes left for Cleveland the next morning. "Take good care of the family," he said to Space Dog.

Space Dog shivered and hoped no one noticed. Mr. Barnes gave Roy and Mrs. Barnes good-bye kisses and drove off to the airport.

Roy spent the afternoon in Space Dog's doghouse. It looked like an office inside, with a desk and a computer. He wanted Space Dog to study the new library book.

"I don't even like the title of this book," said Space Dog. *"How to Turn Your Dog into a Burglar's Worst Enemy.* I'm *afraid* of burglars!"

"I know," said Roy. "Burglars are scary. But think of it this way. Think of all the great stories about dog heroes. Think of Lassie and Benji. Think of all the dogs who protect people. You could be like them—a dog hero who lays his life on the line for the people he loves."

As Roy spoke, Space Dog stood a little taller and straighter beside him. "Yes, I can see it now," said Space Dog. "I could be part of the long tradition of gallant Earth

heroes. Like Paul Revere, or Superman, or the first astronauts..."

Suddenly Space Dog shook his head and came to his senses. "Are you crazy?" he said to Roy. "Now you've got me talking nonsense. I don't *want* to be a hero. I'm just a humble scientist from Queekrg, spending some time on Earth. I wasn't cut out to be a crime stopper."

"It won't be so bad," said Roy. "If you learn a few of the tricks in this book, maybe you'll feel better."

"I learned one good trick on Queekrg," said Space Dog. "One year when I was in school, somebody started stealing my lunch. My mother always packed a really good lunch for me. And the best things in my lunch pack were the pefts."

"What's a peft?" asked Roy.

"It's a yummy dessert. It's like a cake, only rubbery. It's round like a ball, with powdery filling inside."

"It sounds weird," said Roy.

"It was the greatest," said Space Dog. "Anyway, in school we kept our lunches in mini-refrigerators."

"Wow!" said Roy. "Kids had their own refrigerators?"

"Yeah," said Space Dog. "Each student had one under his seat. And this kid who sat next to me, Terg, always managed to get into my fridge and steal my pefts. It was terrible. It was especially terrible because my mother made the best pefts on the planet!"

"So what did you do?" asked Roy.

"I set a trap for the sneaky little devil," said Space Dog. "Before school one day, I sliced open my peft and dumped out all the sugary powder—into my mouth, of course. Then I filled it with the grossest powdery stuff I could think of."

"What was that?" asked Roy.

"Blorp," said Space Dog. "It's a kind of spice. Like garlic, only stronger."

"Yuck!" said Roy.

"Yuck is right," said Space Dog. "I put the peft filled with blorp in my lunch pack and took it to school. Then I put the whole thing in my fridge."

Space Dog smiled. Then he went on. "I didn't see Terg steal the peft, but by noon, when I opened my lunch, it was gone. I sat near Terg in the lunchroom and kept my eye on him. After a while I saw him take a peft out of his lunch pack."

"Then what happened?" asked Roy.

"Some of the other kids noticed that Terg had a peft. He waved it around to make them jealous. Then he opened his mouth wide and took a big bite."

"And?"

"He spat it out—right on the lunch table! It was disgusting. He got into big trouble with the lunch teacher."

"Did he say anything to you?" asked Roy.

"He didn't dare," said Space Dog. "He just gave me a dirty look and drank a lot of garzle juice. But he never stole my pefts again!"

"That was a good story," said Roy. "But I don't think pefts and garzle juice have anything to do with you being a watch-dog."

"I guess not," said Space Dog. "Too

bad. What does it say in that book of yours, anyway?"

3

A Lesson from Blanche

Roy sat on the floor. Space Dog lay on his side, his head propped up with his hand. In that position he did not look much like a dog.

"Let's see," said Roy. "Step one. The book says a good watchdog must be able to sniff out troublemakers."

"Step one is out," said Space Dog. "You know me. The only thing I'm good at sniffing out is food."

He thought for a minute.

"Let's pretend the burglar has already

done something to show he's a trouble-maker. I don't have to sniff him out because I know he's a burglar. He's already tried to get into the house. So what happens next?"

Roy looked at the book. "Step two is to growl at the burglar and try to scare him away. Well, that won't work. We already know you're the world's worst growler."

"Sad but true," said Space Dog.

"Step three is you're supposed to bark," said Roy. "To wake up the people in the house."

Space Dog read aloud over Roy's shoulder. "'The bark acts as an alarm,'" Space Dog read. "'It alerts the dog's owners that there is trouble afoot.' Hoo, boy."

"I've never heard you bark," said Roy. "Do you think you can?"

"Probably not," said Space Dog. "On

Queekrg, if someone goes around barking, everyone thinks he's crazy."

"Most people don't bark here either," said Roy. "But no one thinks twice if a dog barks. And everyone on Earth thinks you're a dog."

"You don't have to remind me," said Space Dog.

"Well, go ahead," said Roy. "Let's hear your bark."

"Oh, Roy," said Space Dog. "This really puts me on the spot. I'm embarrassed."

"There's nothing to be embarrassed about," said Roy. "I don't mind barking. Watch." Roy paused a moment. *Ruff! Ruff!"* he barked. Then he said calmly, "See? Nothing to it!"

"That was good, Roy," said Space Dog. "Now flap your arms like a chicken."

"I don't want to," said Roy.

"Please?" said Space Dog. "If you flap your arms like a chicken, I promise to bark."

"I can't believe this," said Roy. "Okay. Here goes." Roy knelt and bent his arms at the elbow. Then he flapped them like a chicken and said, *"Buck-buck-buck!"*

Space Dog started to laugh, and Roy laughed with him. Suddenly Space Dog stopped laughing. He quickly rolled onto his stomach and pulled up his hind legs. He was trying to look like a dog.

Roy turned around and saw Alice and Blanche peeking in the door of the doghouse.

"Gosh, Roy," said Alice. "What are you doing?"

"Don't you ever knock?" said Roy.

"I didn't know I had to knock," said Alice. "It's just a doghouse. But, wow, you've got a lot of stuff in here." She looked at the stacks of books and papers. Luckily, Space Dog had put his portable computer away.

"This isn't just a doghouse," said Roy. "It's also my secret clubhouse. And you and Blanche are not allowed inside!"

"Okay, okay," said Alice as Roy pushed her out the door. "You don't have to shove."

Roy and Space Dog followed Alice out of the doghouse. Roy closed the door behind them. The minute they were all outside, Blanche walked up to Space Dog, wagging her tail happily.

Slobber was dripping from Blanche's mouth. Space Dog pulled away from her. *Please, Roy!* he begged silently. *Get Blanche out of here!*

It was Alice who came to Space Dog's rescue. "No, Blanche," she said, pulling her dog away. "Space Dog doesn't like to rub noses."

"Thanks, Alice," said Roy. "I'm sorry I got mad about the doghouse. It's just that some things are really secret, you know?"

"I know," said Alice. "But can I ask you

one question?"

"What?"

"Why were you acting like a chicken in there?"

"I was—uh—" Roy stammered. "I was doing some exercises."

"Oh," said Alice. "Well, how's the watchdog training going?"

"Not so well," said Roy.

"I started thinking after we talked yesterday," said Alice. "Blanche needs to learn more about being a watchdog, too. So I taught her some new tricks. Want to see them?"

"Okay," said Roy.

"Well, here goes," said Alice.

Alice held up a sort of rag doll made of old socks. The sock doll had a face drawn on with Magic Marker.

"I made this," said Alice. "It's supposed

to be a burglar. Now watch."

Alice shook the doll in Blanche's face and said in a low, mean voice, "Heh, heh, heh! I'm a horrible burglar, and I'm coming to rob your house!"

Blanche began to growl.

Alice threw the sock doll on the ground. "Get the burglar, Blanche!" she said. "Get him, girl!"

Growling, Blanche pounced on the doll. She grabbed it with her teeth and began to tear it up. "Isn't she great?" said Alice. "The only bad thing is that I have to keep making new dolls. Blanche rips them to shreds."

"Wow!" said Roy. "She really has a killer instinct. Or else she just likes tearing up socks."

Space Dog was watching Blanche. He rolled his eyes. *That poodle is an idiot*, he

thought to himself. *She fights socks as though they were going to fight her back.*

Alice went to Blanche and tried to get the burglar doll away from her. "Give it to me, Blanchie," she said.

But Blanche held on. Alice tugged, but her dog would not let go.

Finally Alice had to force Blanche's mouth open. The sock doll fell to the ground. By then, it was nothing but rags.

Alice picked it up and handed it to Roy.

"Want to try the burglar with Space Dog?" she asked.

Roy hesitated. "Well…"

"Come on," said Alice. "Try it. Maybe Space Dog will surprise you."

"Okay," said Roy. He shook what was left of the burglar doll in front of Space Dog. Little droplets flew off it. "It's kind of wet," said Roy.

Space Dog's stomach turned. He knew why the rags were wet. They had been in Blanche's mouth.

Roy held the beat-up doll closer and closer to Space Dog. "Here comes a burglar, Space Dog," he said. "He's coming to get you!"

Space Dog started to back away from Roy. The closer Roy came, the more Space

Dog backed away. Finally Roy tossed the burglar on the ground and said, "Sic 'em, Space Dog!"

Space Dog looked up at Roy. Then he sat down quietly.

"Wow," said Alice. "He really is a hopeless case, isn't he?"

"Yeah," said Roy. "But I like him anyway."

4

Space Dog's
First Night on the Job

Roy and Space Dog sat in Roy's room after supper.

"Well," said Roy, "tonight's your first night on duty." He tried to sound cheerful.

Space Dog looked miserable. "What if something goes wrong?" he said. "I'm a heavy sleeper. A burglar could clean the house out, and I would probably sleep through it."

"No way," said Roy. "But we won't take any chances. Let's figure out just what you have to do. First of all, you have to stay downstairs all night."

"What?" said Space Dog. "By myself?"

"Well…"

"Alone?" said Space Dog with horror in his voice.

Roy thought quickly. Space Dog was getting upset. If he got too upset, he might leave. He might fix his little spaceship and fly off. Roy couldn't let that happen.

"I'll stay downstairs with you," said Roy. "At least for tonight."

"Good," said Space Dog. He sounded relieved. "What do we do if a burglar comes?"

"You bark, I guess," Roy answered.

"I'd better practice," said Space Dog. "How does it go again?"

"Ruff! Ruff!" barked Roy.

"Bark, bark," said Space Dog. "How

was that?"

"No good," said Roy. "Worse than your growl."

"What am I going to do?" said Space Dog. "I'm scared."

"If we're together, you won't be scared," said Roy.

Space Dog smiled at him. "You're right," he said. "You're a pal, Roy. Thank you."

"No problem," said Roy. "I always wanted to spend the night downstairs. But we'll have to be very quiet. Mom will kill me if she catches me out of bed."

"Okay," said Space Dog. "We'll be quiet." Suddenly he thought of a new problem. "Roy, do watchdogs stay awake all night?"

Roy sighed. "I think they're supposed to," he said.

"I can't do that," said Space Dog. "I'm sure I'll fall asleep."

"Don't worry," Roy said quickly. "I'll help you stay awake. It won't be so hard."

Roy patted his friend and sighed. He wanted to keep Space Dog happy. But he was afraid he wasn't doing a very good job.

That night Space Dog stayed downstairs when Roy went up to bed. Mrs. Barnes kissed Roy good night and turned off the light. Then she went back downstairs.

Roy lay in the dark, trying to stay awake. He waited forever for his mother to go to bed.

At last Mrs. Barnes turned out the lights in the living room and started upstairs. "Good night, Space Dog," she said. "Guard us well!"

Space Dog moaned.

A few minutes later, Roy got out of bed and tiptoed down the stairs. The whole house was dark. When he got downstairs, he whispered, "Psst! Space Dog!"

"Over here!" Space Dog whispered back. He was in the living room.

Roy joined him on the sofa. "How's it going?" he asked.

"Okay," said Space Dog. "But I'm already sleepy. And it's only eleven o'clock!"

The two friends sat in the dark, saying nothing. The clock on the mantelpiece went *tick, tick, tick*. The refrigerator hummed in the kitchen.

Everything else was quiet.

"What should we do?" Roy whispered.

"I don't know," said Space Dog. "But we have to find something to keep us

awake."

"Should we play a game?" asked Roy.

"Too dark," said Space Dog.

"Should we watch TV?" asked Roy.

"Too noisy," said Space Dog.

They sat on the sofa, twiddling their thumbs. Space Dog yawned.

"Maybe we can turn on a teensy, weensy little light somewhere," said Space Dog. "Let's find a teensy light."

They settled on a reading lamp in the den. Space Dog waited while Roy found some sheets of paper. Then Roy showed Space Dog how to make paper airplanes. Once they finished a plane, they flew it quietly over the rug.

In the middle of making planes, Space Dog suddenly froze.

"What's wrong?" asked Roy.

"Did you hear that?" said Space Dog.

"What?"

"That noise," said Space Dog.

"What noise?"

Just then there was a little crash. It sounded like metal.

"*That* noise," said Space Dog.

"Yikes!" said Roy. "What is it?"

"I don't know," said Space Dog. "It came from the back of the house."

They heard the sound again, this time a little louder. Space Dog and Roy grabbed each other.

"Is this it?" said Space Dog. "Is the burglar here?"

"I don't know," said Roy. "You'd better go look."

"*Me?*" said Space Dog. "Why me?"

"You're the watchdog," said Roy.

Crash. Bump. Then there was the sound of paper rustling.

"Help!" whispered Space Dog. "What should we do?"

"Let's both go see what it is," said Roy.

"Okay," said Space Dog.

Still holding on to each other, Space Dog and Roy tiptoed into the dark kitchen. They heard more noises—coming from outside the back door. Something or someone was definitely out there!

5

Who's There?

Space Dog and Roy tiptoed over to the kitchen window and slowly peeked out. A garbage can was tipped over. Something furry had its head inside the can.

"What's that?" whispered Space Dog.

"It's not a burglar," said Roy. "It's just a raccoon. That's an animal that gets into people's garbage."

Space Dog breathed a sigh of relief. "Is that all?" he said. "Thank goodness. Let's go back to the den."

"Wait," said Roy. "Maybe raccoons are

supposed to be part of your job. They leave trash all over the yard. Go chase him away."

"*You* chase him away," said Space Dog. "He's pretty big."

"Well, we've got to do something," said Roy.

"What about the paper airplanes?" said Space Dog. "They're nice and pointy. We

could aim them at the raccoon."

"And they don't make any noise," said Roy. "Good idea."

He and Space Dog went back to the den. They got a stack of airplanes and took them into the kitchen. Then they quietly opened the back door.

The raccoon didn't even look up. He was busy with the garbage. Space Dog and

Roy stood in the doorway and aimed. Roy threw the first plane. It missed.

Then Space Dog tried. His plane bopped the raccoon's side. "Got him!" said Space Dog. The raccoon looked up. His eyes glowed yellow.

Roy threw another plane. It landed at the raccoon's feet. The animal backed up a little.

After a few more airplanes, the raccoon finally got the message. He waddled away to dig in someone else's garbage. Roy and Space Dog shook hands.

"Let's play Old Maid," said Space Dog. "I'll get the cards."

"Not yet," said Roy. "We have to clean up first."

"You mean go out there and pick up that garbage?" said Space Dog.

"Yes," Roy insisted. "My mother is

going to think it's weird if the yard is covered with garbage and paper airplanes."

Quiet as mice, they crept outside and picked up the garbage. When they were finished, they went inside and locked the door behind them.

"I've got to wash up," said Space Dog.

"Okay," said Roy. "But do it really, really quietly."

They washed their hands in a trickle of water at the kitchen sink. Then they found the cards and tiptoed back to the den. Many hours and many card games later, the sky began to grow light.

"I'd better go upstairs now," said Roy. "It's almost morning. My mom will be getting up. Will you be okay by yourself now?"

"Yes," said Space Dog. "As long as it's light outside, I'm not scared. Burglars don't usually come in the morning, do they?"

"I don't think so," said Roy. "Well, see you later."

"See you," said Space Dog.

Roy tiptoed upstairs to his room. He got into bed and fell asleep before his head hit the pillow.

An hour later, Mrs. Barnes woke up. When she went downstairs to start the coffee, she found her watchdog sound asleep.

6

Sleepy Sunday

That morning Roy slept and slept. Even though it was Sunday and he didn't have to get up, his mother began to think that he was sick. Finally she went to his room to wake him.

"Roy?" said Mrs. Barnes. "Roy?"

Roy only turned in his sleep.

"Roy?" Mrs. Barnes shook her son lightly.

Roy opened his eyes. "What? Is there a burglar?" he said.

"No, honey," said Mrs. Barnes. "No bur-

glar. I was just wondering if you were all right."

"Oh," said Roy. He rubbed his eyes and sat up in bed. "I'm all right," he said. "Just tired."

"That's not like you," said Mrs. Barnes. "Are you sure you're not sick?"

"No, no!" said Roy, thinking quickly. "It's probably just, you know, getting used to school again and everything."

Mrs. Barnes felt Roy's forehead. "You don't feel hot," she said. "But tonight you're going to bed early, young man. You've got school tomorrow, you know."

"I know, Mom," said Roy. "I promise to get a good night's sleep tonight."

"Good boy," said Mrs. Barnes. "Now come downstairs and have some lunch. Or breakfast, if you want."

"Okay," said Roy.

When Roy went downstairs, he saw Space Dog asleep on the living room floor. *I'd like to curl up next to him*, Roy thought with a yawn.

The smell of spaghetti and meatballs woke Space Dog before supper. He walked into the kitchen just as Roy and his mother were sitting down to eat. Roy's face lit up when he saw Space Dog.

"Hi, old pal," said Roy.

Space Dog gave Roy a wink as he walked through the kitchen. Then he went out through the swinging dog door to the backyard.

After supper Roy took some leftover spaghetti out to the doghouse. He knocked his secret code on the doghouse door— two slow knocks and two fast.

"I smell supper," Space Dog said.

"Come in."

Roy crawled into the doghouse. "Hi, Space Dog," he said, handing over the food. "I'm glad you're up. I missed you this afternoon."

"Well, now we have all night together," said Space Dog. "I'm ready to whip you in another round of Old Maid." He speared a meatball with his fork and popped it into his mouth. "Mmm," he said. "My compliments to the chef."

Roy was sitting cross-legged. He looked down at his sneakers. "There's one little problem," he said. "I can't stay with you tonight. I've got school tomorrow."

Space Dog stopped eating and looked at Roy. "You mean I have to stay up all night by myself?" He dropped his fork. "I just lost my appetite."

"Don't feel bad, Space Dog," said Roy.

"Don't feel bad?" Space Dog echoed. "What's there to feel good about? It won't be any fun staying up all night without you. And besides, it's *scary!*"

"Maybe it's okay if you go to sleep tonight," said Roy. "As long as you're downstairs."

"Thank goodness," said Space Dog. "But I still have to stay by myself, right?"

"Right," said Roy.

Space Dog looked unhappy again. Roy tried to think of a way to make him feel better. "As soon as my father gets home," he said, "I'll tell him you have to sleep in my room again—because I just can't sleep without you!"

7

Space Dog Stands Alone

Roy and Space Dog were in Roy's room. Roy was getting ready for bed.

"It's not fair," said Space Dog, watching Roy get into his pajamas. "You get to sleep in a nice warm bed. I have to go downstairs and play watchdog. What a world."

Just then there was a knock on the bedroom door. "Come in," said Roy.

It was Mrs. Barnes. "Almost ready for bed, Roy?" she said.

"Yes, Mom," said Roy.

"Good," said Mrs. Barnes. "I'll take the

dog downstairs. Come on, Space Dog. Out you go."

Space Dog gave Roy his saddest look. Then Mrs. Barnes shooed him out of the room.

"Good night, Space Dog," Roy called after him.

Sleep tight, Roy, you lucky duck, Space Dog thought to himself.

For the next two nights, Roy slept upstairs while Space Dog dozed on the floor downstairs. Poor Space Dog would wake up from time to time, hearing one kind of noise or another. He began having bad dreams. During the day he was tired and cranky. Roy was worried about him.

On Wednesday night, Space Dog waited downstairs as usual while Mrs. Barnes turned on the dishwasher and turned off the lights. It wasn't long before she went upstairs to bed. Soon the house was as quiet as a church.

Space Dog made his rounds. He dragged himself from room to room. He checked the windows and doors to make sure they were locked.

Now what? he wondered. *I know. A little solitaire.*

Space Dog sat on the floor and played cards. He played game after game. But he couldn't seem to win. He was lonesome for Roy.

He was just getting up to fix himself a little snack when he heard a noise. He froze. His heart pounded madly. But he told himself to calm down. *It's probably just another raccoon,* he thought. *Don't panic.*

The house was still. Space Dog listened for more noises. Then he heard something that sounded like footsteps coming up the front walk.

Space Dog hugged himself hard. *Oh, no!* he thought. *I'm too young to die! Somebody do something!*

Space Dog was standing in the front hall of the house. Suddenly he saw the doorknob begin to turn. *Help!* thought Space Dog. *It's a burglar trying to get in! I have to stop him!*

The doorknob rattled. Quickly Space Dog shoved the hall table in front of the door.

Quick! What would a watchdog do? Space Dog screamed to himself.

Then he answered himself. *Who cares what a watchdog would do!* he thought. *I'm calling the police!*

He raced to the kitchen and dialed

911. "Get me the police!" he whispered into the phone. He gave the Barneses' address.

"We already have a car in the area," said the operator. "The officers should arrive any minute."

"Thank you!" said Space Dog, and he hung up the phone. He peeked into the hallway. The intruder had unlocked the door. He was slowly pushing it open, but the table was in the way.

The robber started ringing the door-bell. "Hey!" he shouted. "Will somebody let me in?"

A chill ran down Space Dog's spine. He knew that voice. That was no robber! That was Mr. Barnes!

Then Space Dog heard a siren. *Oh, no!* he thought. *Here come the police!*

He watched out the window as a

police car pulled up in front of the house. Two officers ran up the front walk and grabbed Mr. Barnes.

Space Dog darted to the front door and pulled the table away from it. The door swung open. Mr. Barnes was shouting at the police officers. "What are you doing? This is my house!"

Roy and Mrs. Barnes both came running downstairs. "Barney!" cried Mrs. Barnes when she saw her husband and the police. "*What* is going on?"

"Excuse us, ma'am," said one of the police officers. "We caught this man breaking into your house."

"Breaking in?" said Mrs. Barnes. "But he lives here!"

"He does?" said the officer.

"That's what I was trying to tell you!" huffed Mr. Barnes.

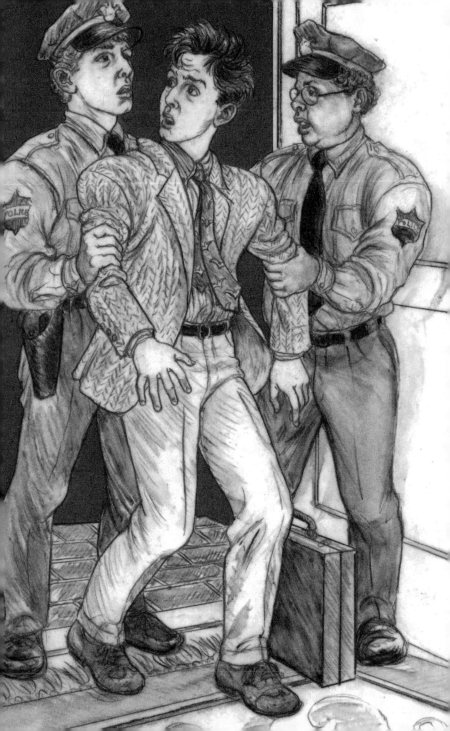

The two officers looked confused. "But someone called us and reported a break-in," said the second officer.

Roy looked at Space Dog. Space Dog shrugged. He stared at the ceiling.

Mrs. Barnes went up to Mr. Barnes and kissed him. "Officers, this is my husband," she said. "You can release him."

The policemen had been holding Mr. Barnes by the arm. "We're very sorry," said the first officer, letting him go. "I guess there was a mistake."

"I don't know which crazy neighbor made that call," said Mr. Barnes, "but you jumped to conclusions pretty fast."

"That's all right," said Mrs. Barnes. "We know the police were just doing their job. Right, Barney?"

Mr. Barnes rubbed his arm. "Right," he said. "But next time, be careful before you start grabbing people!"

"Yes, sir. Sorry, sir," said the policemen. "Good night."

The police officers left. Mr. Barnes picked up his suitcase and went inside the house. Mrs. Barnes and Roy hugged him.

"Welcome home, Dad!" said Roy.

"What a night!" said Mr. Barnes. Then he saw Space Dog. "By the way, what has *he* been doing all this time?" he said. "I could have been a burglar for all this dog knew, but he didn't bark once. Some watchdog!"

"That's not right, Dad," said Roy. "Space Dog took good care of us while you were gone. Didn't he, Mom?"

"I guess so, honey," said Mrs. Barnes. "It's hard to say."

"He did," said Roy. "I know he did."

"It doesn't matter," said Mr. Barnes.

"We don't need a watchdog anymore."

"We don't?" said Roy happily. Space Dog's ears perked up.

"No," said Mr. Barnes. "I've decided to put in a burglar alarm."

"You have?" said Mrs. Barnes.

"Yes," said Mr. Barnes.

"Can Space Dog sleep in my room again?" said Roy.

"I don't see why not," said Mrs. Barnes.

"Hurray!" said Roy.

"Speaking of sleep," said Mrs. Barnes, "it's awfully late. You'd better get to bed, Roy."

Roy kissed his parents good night. Then he and Space Dog went upstairs.

Once they were alone together, settling into bed, Roy said to Space Dog, "You called the police, didn't you?"

"Yes," said Space Dog. "I didn't know

your father was coming home tonight. I thought he was a burglar. What a lousy watchdog I am!"

"No, you're not," said Roy. "You're the greatest! You stayed up all night just to keep us safe. It's not your fault there wasn't a real burglar. If a burglar *had* come, you would have been a hero."

"Maybe you're right," said Space Dog. "If your dad had been a burglar, I would have helped catch him. Then I would have been a hero."

"Of course I'm right," said Roy sleepily.

Space Dog snuggled down under the covers. "I'm glad I don't have to be a watchdog anymore," he said. "It's good to be back in my own cozy bed."

8

The Burglar Alarm

The very next day while Roy was at school, the burglar alarm people came and put in the new system. Mr. Barnes stayed home from the office to watch the alarm being installed. When Roy came home, his father showed him how it worked.

"I bought the fanciest system they had," said Mr. Barnes as he played with the buttons and lights. "But remember, it's not a toy."

"Right," said Roy.

Mr. Barnes pointed to a little hole in

the wall at the bottom of the stairs. "When the alarm is on," he said, "a laser beam will shoot out of here. If anybody tries to walk up the stairs at night, the alarm will go off. You got that?"

"Right, Dad," said Roy.

Mrs. Barnes came out of the kitchen. "I've just finished calling all the neighbors," she said. "One or two say they heard the sirens last night, but not one of them called the police."

"Whoever called doesn't want to admit it," said Mr. Barnes. "They don't want to look silly."

"You may be right, dear," said Roy's mother.

"Dad," said Roy, "can I go out and play now?"

"You haven't done your homework yet," said Mr. Barnes.

"I'll do it later," said Roy.

"Oh, no, you won't," said Mr. Barnes. "You'll march upstairs and do it right now."

"Dad!" said Roy.

"Barney," said Mrs. Barnes. "Let him go outside. He needs a chance to relax after last night. It's frightening to have the police arrive at midnight—even if it was a false alarm."

"Oh, all right," said Mr. Barnes. "I'm sorry, Roy. Go on out and play."

"Thanks, Dad," said Roy. He ran through the kitchen and out the back door. He saw Alice and Blanche playing next door.

"Hi, Roy!" called Alice. "Watch this!" She tossed a doggy treat up in the air. Blanche jumped up high, wiggled three times like a hula dancer, and caught the treat. Then she ate it.

"Great, huh?" said Alice.

"Yeah," said Roy. "That's a good trick."

"I bet Space Dog can't do that," said Alice.

"I bet you're right," said Roy.

"I bet you wish he *could* do it," said Alice.

"Not really," said Roy. "There are other things I like about Space Dog."

"Like what?" asked Alice.

"For one thing, he doesn't drool," said Roy.

That made Alice mad. She threw a doggy treat at Roy. "You dodo," she said. "Dogs are *supposed* to drool."

"Maybe so," said Roy. "But it's nicer when they don't. See you."

"See you, Roy."

Roy knocked his secret knock on the doghouse door. "Come in," said Space Dog.

Roy went in on all fours. "Hi," he said. "What are you doing?"

"I'm reading the encyclopedia. The section about crime on earth. I figure I have firsthand experience with it now."

Roy shook his head. "I wish I could tell Alice what an amazing dog you are," he said. "She was just showing off with Blanche again."

"I know," said Space Dog. "But that's the way it goes. Just think of me the way you think of Superman."

"What do you mean?" asked Roy.

"Well," said Space Dog, "*we* know I'm special, like Superman. But Alice thinks I'm just ordinary, like Clark Kent. Get it?"

"Hmm," said Roy. "I never thought of it that way before."

That night the Barnes family went to bed

early. But Space Dog had trouble getting to sleep. Staying up half the night for most of the week had thrown him off schedule.

He listened to Roy's slow, steady breathing and knew Roy was asleep. He went out in the hall and heard the low rumble of Mr. Barnes's snores.

I know what I need, thought Space Dog. *A little snack.*

Space Dog tiptoed down the stairs, trying not to make them creak. But when he got to the foot of the stairs...

RRRRRIIIIINNNNNNNGGGGG!!!!

All the Barneses ran out into the upstairs hallway. "Call the police!" shouted Mr. Barnes. Roy looked down and saw Space Dog shaking at the bottom of the stairs. Mrs. Barnes saw him, too. She calmly went to a box on the wall and switched off the alarm. The house was suddenly

quiet.

"Calm down, Barney," said Mrs. Barnes. "Look." She pointed to Space Dog. "It's not a burglar. It's our watchdog."

Space Dog lay down and put his paws over his eyes. Roy went downstairs to pat him.

"But Space Dog couldn't have gotten in the way of that laser beam," said Mr. Barnes. "I made sure it was set high enough so that he could go underneath."

Roy's heart gave a thump. He knew Space Dog must have set off the alarm by walking like a person, on two feet. Maybe his father would finally guess there was something strange going on.

But Mr. Barnes just threw up his hands. "That dog," he said sleepily, heading back to bed. "Nothing but trouble."

Roy patted Space Dog. "Dad thinks

you're Clark Kent," he said. "But don't worry. I know you're Superman."

It's a dog's life on earth!
But Space Dog puts up with it for his
new best friend, a human boy called Roy.

SPACE DOG AND ROY
When a spaceship crashes in his backyard,
Roy gets what he's always wanted—a dog of
his very own!

SPACE DOG AND THE PET SHOW
Space Dog agrees to enter a pet show for
Roy's sake. But he didn't bargain on a beauty
makeover at Dottie's Dog Salon!

SPACE DOG IN TROUBLE
A weekend at Granny's for Roy and his parents means a vacation for Space Dog—until
he's dog-napped by the dogcatcher!

SPACE DOG THE HERO
Roy's dad insists that Space Dog guard the
house. But Space Dog is a hopeless watchdog—he can't even growl!

About the Author

NATALIE STANDIFORD has often wondered if animals aren't secretly smarter than we think they are. She's sure that kids know a lot more than adults think they do. When she wrote about Space Dog, she imagined that he'd feel the way a lot of kids feel—misunderstood.

Natalie has written several books about dogs, but at home in New York City she has a cat, Iggy. So far, Iggy hasn't inspired any books. But you never know...

About the Illustrator

KATHLEEN COLLINS HOWELL began drawing pictures at age four and went on to study art in college. Today she is an illustrator of many books for children.

Kathleen and her husband, Jack, live half the year in Buffalo, New York, and half the year in rural England.